This book belongs to

....

For my darling Nathaniel, so, so much.

And for my nephews Leo and Orion,
two of the hungriest little lions I know.

SIMON AND SCHUSTER
First published in Great Britain in 2016
by Simon and Schuster UK Ltd
1st Floor, 222 Gray's Inn Road, London, WC1X 8HB
A CBS Company

Originally published by Atheneum,
an imprint of Simon and Schuster Children's Publishing Division,
New York in 2016

Text and illustrations copyright © 2016 Lucy Ruth Cummins

A CIP catalogue record for this book is available
from the British Library upon request

978-1-4711-4707-4 (PB)

Printed in China

1 3 5 7 9 10 8 6 4 2

A HUNGRY LION

or a dwindling assortment of animals

written and illustrated by

Lucy Ruth Cummins

SIMON AND SCHUSTER
London   New York   Sydney   Toronto   New Delhi

Once upon a time there was a hungry lion,
a penguin, a turtle, a little calico kitten,
a brown mouse, a bunny with floppy ears
and a bunny with un-floppy ears,
a frog, a bat, a pig, a slightly bigger pig,
a woolly sheep, a koala, and also a hen.

Hold on.

O nce upon a time there was a hungry lion,

a penguin, a turtle, a brown mouse,

those two rabbits –

one with ears that flopped,

one with ears that did not –

a frog, a bat, a regular-sized pig, a koala and a hen.

Wait a second.

It seems there was *just* a hungry lion,
a turtle, only the floppy-eared rabbit,
a frog, a bat, and a pig.
And apparently . . .

. . . no one else.

Umm . . .

I guess . . .

Once upon a time
there was just a
HUNGRY LION

and a dwindling assortment
of other animals.

Well. Okay . . . It seems now we have only

A HUNGRY LION

. . . and that turtle.

Hello, there. *Excuse me* –
where did everyone go?

Ummm . . .

HEY!

'Why's it so dark in here??'

shhhhhh . . .

Hooray!

Once upon a time there was an
enormous, lovely four-tiered cake
with buttercream frosting,
a partying penguin, a twisting turtle,
a calico kitten — who happens
to be shimmying — a brown mouse
(a bit of a wallflower),
two bunnies line-dancing, a sheep chatting
with a frog, a bat doing his bat thing, a pair
of pigs squealing with piggish delight,
a contented koala, a happy hen . . .

and . . .

. . . a less hungry lion.

Well, look who's arrived
fashionably late.
A really ravenous T. rex!

Once upon a time
there was just a
hungry little turtle . . .

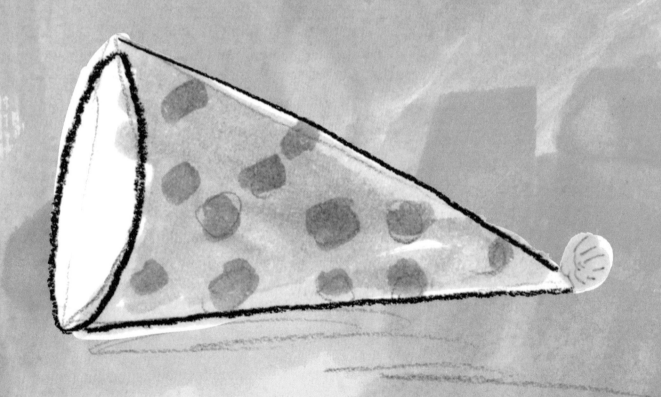

. . . and a very large cake.

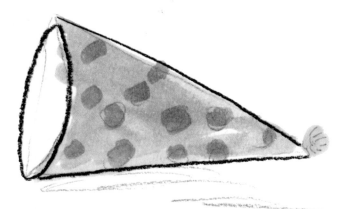